Littles

by CarrieAnn Reda

Pigs Might Fly

Fly fly humming-pig,
Buzzing through the air,
Fly fly humming-pig,
To all the flowers fair.

The Journey

Over and under, under and over,
Traveling through branch and moss,
Under and over, over and under,
Even small journeys are a wonder.

Follow Your Guiding Light

Follow your guiding light,

Through storm, through fog,

through night,

No matter how high the stormy

waves may go,

Your guiding light will always show.

Fortune Favors the Brave

It does not matter what you face,

Or what is facing you.

The only thing you can embrace,

Is what you're going to do.

Friendship Takes Courage

Some friends are feathered,
Some friends are furry,
Some friends may fly,
And some friends may scurry.

Hedge and go Seek

When I'm in a prickly mood,
I like to find somewhere prickly to
brood,
A prickly place to be,
Is fine for a prickly me.

Sleepy Fox

Away away in peaceful sleep,

Sheltered by moss and tree,

Rocked by nature's gentle hand,

Away away to dreaming land.

Little Wishes

Big dreams may find their way

In the landscape of our everyday,

But chasing them may make us blue,

As we forget our little wishes do

come true.

Some Bunny to Love

All the beautiful twinkling stars
Set in the sapphire sky far above,
Twinkle and sparkle so prettily,
Shine brighter with some bunny
to love.

Owl Always Love You

There is a place next to me,
A place for you always to be,
Yet, even if we are apart,
There is a place for you always in my
heart.